Old Home Day

BROWNDEER PRESS · HARCOURT BRACE & COMPANY

San Diego   New York   London

Donald Hall

Old Home Day

ILLUSTRATED BY

Emily Arnold McCully

Requests for permission to make copies of any part of the work should
be mailed to: Permissions Department, Harcourt Brace & Company,
6277 Sea Harbor Drive, Orlando, Florida 32887-6777.

Browndeer Press is a registered trademark of Harcourt Brace & Company.

Library of Congress Cataloging-in-Publication Data
Hall, Donald, 1928–
Old Home Day/by Donald Hall; illustrated by Emily Arnold McCully.
p. cm.
"Browndeer Press."
Summary: The story of the growth of a fictional New Hampshire village
from prehistory to the bicentennial celebration of its founding.
ISBN 0-15-276896-3
[1. Blackwater (N.H.)—Fiction.] I. McCully, Emily Arnold, ill. II. Title.
PZ7.H411501 1996
[E]—dc20 93-3658

First edition A B C D E

Printed in Singapore

For Dick Smart

—D. H.

WHEN the ice mountain melted north, it scraped trenches and dents in the valleys between the hills. It left boulders behind and ice that became water, and filled dents making ponds and trenches making rivers.

So Blackwater Pond began, although nobody called it Blackwater Pond for tens of thousands of years. And nobody would call this land New Hampshire for tens of thousands of years.

Grasses and shrubs came to Blackwater Pond, and insects, and fish.

Birds were summer visitors then. Some of them brought seeds in their feathers. Birches grew around Blackwater Pond, and hemlock, and oak, and elm. For thousands of years maple trees reddened in the cold autumn and nobody saw them. Winter froze the pond and nobody noticed.

In the spring the birds came back, deer nibbled new leaves, and bears woke up.

Ten thousand years ago the first people came in summer, like the birds. They pitched tepees by the pond and made fishhooks out of bone and fished there. They carved arrowheads and shot deer with bows and arrows.

Later trappers came, who trapped beaver and sent furs across the ocean to London and Paris.

Sometimes the arrow makers and the trappers made friends and helped each other.
Sometimes they fought each other.
After a long war up north, the old tribes of arrow makers retreated west.

Still, birds came back every summer.
Still, ice froze in the winter and bears slept in their caves.

In 1799 Enoch Boswell was looking for a place to build a cabin, keep a cow, and raise a family. He came upon a pond brimming with dark water.

He built a cabin by the pond and planted corn. When he found arrowheads he tossed them aside.

Enoch went back to Cambridge near Boston and married his sweetheart, Arianna, and brought her to his cabin.

Benjamin was born there, and Elzira, and Nathan, and Olan, and Edna, and Lucy, and Artelia, and Chastity, and John.

Enoch and Arianna called their twenty acres of water Blackwater Pond.

So did their grandchildren, who farmed a dozen places near Blackwater Village in the town of Blackwater by the year 1840.

Some cousins quarreled and called themselves Bussell instead of Boswell.

The Lovells moved up from Portsmouth, and the McIntoshes from Worcester, and the Wittleseas all the way from Connecticut.

Each family kept a mooly cow for milk to drink or to turn into butter and cheese.
Each family kept a horse, and a pair of oxen, and sheep, and pigs, and chickens—
and each tended a big garden. Each family grew all its vegetables and fruits: peas,
rhubarb, apples, corn, beets, potatoes, pears, squash, pumpkins, beans, and parsnips.

The farmers boiled sap into maple syrup and maple sugar in the spring.

They picked berries on the mountain in the summer.

They slaughtered a pig every autumn and ate salt pork and smoked ham all winter.

They sheared sheep, carded wool, spun it, wove it, and made their own clothes.

They grew flax, made linen, and made more clothes.

Twice a year they made soap.

Once in a while somebody left Blackwater Pond to go as far as New Hampshire's
state capital, Concord.

They came back as soon as they could.

Farmers cut down half the trees in the forest around Blackwater Pond to clear the land.

Achille Lebeau came down from Canada to chop wood, then settled in Blackwater to farm. His cousin Felix Letourneau followed him.

Wesley Winters set up as a blacksmith. Peter Lovewell built a tavern, where his wife, Priscilla, cooked for travelers.

Amos Buswell built a sawmill on the Black River. Then he built a gristmill. Then he started a bank for all the farmers who had settled in Blackwater by 1840, when the town numbered four hundred and seventy-five people.

Every March a hundred and twenty men sat for Town Meeting.

In 1850 the railroad came, but Blackwater Village was hilly, so the depot was built four miles from the pond, near the village of East Stubbtown.

Farmers in the valley, close to the railroad, bred holsteins and sold their milk to travel by rail down to Concord or even to Manchester.

Charles Whittlesea started a fishmonger's, Luther Lowe a livery stable, Algernon Bussett a butcher shop, and David and Lucille Laboud a general store.

Farmers around the pond kept on in the old way. Some sons and daughters left the hard life for work in Buswell's Mills, or even the mills of Manchester or Lowell. In the mills, you worked only seventy-two hours a week.

When Johnny Reb fired on Fort Sumter, the young men enlisted. Like everybody else, Fred Bosell knew that the Union would win the war in six months. He'd be home in time to help with the harvest.

When he came back to Blackwater four years later, he was no longer a boy. His best friend, Ebenezer McIntosh, stayed at Shiloh forever. Fergus Whittleseth never left Libby Prison.

Through subscription the town raised a monument to the Union soldier, in bronze, with twenty-seven names listed on the side. Four names had gold stars beside them.

Restless in Blackwater, Fred Bosell married a Lowell girl, and they moved to Ohio.

Once, when he was an old man, he came back for the Fourth of July. He umpired the baseball game between Blackwater's married and single men.

More and more people left Blackwater every year. Enoch Boswell's old place by the pond, empty after his great-great-great-granddaughter Hester settled in Oregon, stood for a dozen years.

The blizzard of 1888 collapsed the roof in.

Birch trees grew from Enoch's cellar hole.

Old men kept farming, and when their widows died, the houses and barns caved in and the fields grew up to pine. Only stone walls marked where Felix Letourneau once kept sheep and pigs.

In summer old Blackwater people came back like the birds. They brought their grandchildren to show them where the barn was—and where they had gone to the one-room school.

In 1899 the governor proclaimed Old Home Day, so that everybody who had moved away from New Hampshire could come back home at the same time and visit.

First Selectman Harold Buswall proclaimed Blackwater's first Old Home Day, setting the date for the last weekend in August 1899, just a hundred years after Enoch had built his cabin.

Tom Buzzle came up with his family from Lowell, Massachusetts, for Blackwater's Old Home and Centenary, alighting from the depot at East Stubbtown and taking the stagecoach up to the town hall with its little green.

He met Bridie Love there, who had been sweet on him when they were nine years old. He tipped his cap to Selectman Buswall, the biggest farmer still in town. He drank cider with Buster Lowe and Toot Labelle, who never left town because that's where the cider was. He stayed up half the night telling stories with Hamish and Ruth Whittlesaw, who had taken the train all the way from North Carolina.

At the end of World War I, Blackwater added a small plaque to its Civil War monument, with the names of five boys who went to war. Four came back, but three of them moved to Massachusetts.

When children went south to college, they married and stayed in the city.

In the 1930s only two hundred people lived in Blackwater; in the 1940s there were only a hundred and sixty. The woods came back where the farms had been.

Three trailers roosted near the pond. Beside one of them, old man Bostell kept his collection of rusted Fords and Chevys.

The last weekend of August during those years, Blackwater birds flew back for Old Home Day. In the church on Sunday, the town gave prizes for the largest family, the youngest, the oldest—and the family that came from the farthest away.

The people who had stayed presented a play for the people who had come back. Everybody went to the Old Home Day dance.

Albert Bosell from Ohio, grandson of Fred, the Civil War veteran, won every year for traveling the greatest distance.

In 1952 two families bought land by the pond and built summer cottages. In 1955 Brent Boswill built a motel where Route 102 crosses Blackwater Road. By 1965 fifty summer people came to Blackwater.

At the end of each August, the new people attended Old Home Day in their new place. They started the Blackwater Historical Association, which met during the summer.

Town Meeting argued all night, then voted funds to clean up the junkyard after old man Bostell died.

By 1970 the old Amos Buswell place was restored, tidy and handsome, by a sculptor from Idaho named Linda Zuckerman.

By 1972 seven old farmhouses looked almost new, freshly painted and spruced up.

By 1980 three hundred people lived in Blackwater again, at least in the summer, and Blackwater's young men carpentered new houses.

Sometimes when they dug foundations they found arrowheads, which they displayed on their mantels at home.

In 1995 the selectmen planned Blackwater's bicentennial for the last weekend of August in 1999.

The whole town would wear 1799 costumes and ride in a parade of buggies and eat together and dance on the village green.

Visitors from their sister village of Elva in Estonia would fly over to visit, if they could. Selectman Costello would ask Town Meeting for travel money.

In August of 1999 Edward Boswell and his wife, Adrienne, came to Old Home Day when she was seven months pregnant with their first child. Some neighbors of theirs in Boston had told them how beautiful Blackwater was.

They ate red flannel hash in the food tent.

They threw horseshoes.

They inspected fancywork and bought booties.

They admired the exhibition of blacksmithing and the parade with the Andover Lions stagecoach.

They thought, *Maybe sometime we can live in this beautiful place.*

They didn't know it, but their baby would be Enoch Boswell's great-great-great-great-great-great-great-great-grandchild.

"What shall we call him, if he's a boy?" asked Edward.

Adrienne caught sight of the historic plaque on the town hall. "Let's call him Enoch," she said.

Author's Note

It was Old Home *Week* when it started, proclaimed by New Hampshire Governor Frank Rollins in 1899. Like the little towns, it has shrunk.

Today most Americans live in urban places, cities and suburbs that have expanded as our nation's population has increased. Old neighborhoods have become sites of constant change. When middle-aged people return to the streets of childhood, often they find houses and stores torn down, replaced by condominiums, supermarkets, malls, and parking lots.

I live in the New Hampshire countryside, where from my front porch I can see only one other house. I walk my dog on a narrow dirt lane called New Canada Road, overarched by great oaks and bordered with clumps of white birch trees. I walk through a dense mixed forest, regularly logged—but stone walls still edge the road, barriers erected a hundred and fifty years ago to keep cattle or sheep in the cleared pastures. I walk past cellar holes of houses where farmers lived who chopped and burned the original trees to make space for garden, hayfield, and pasture.

When our country was new, people flocked from New England's Atlantic coast to the northern fields to farm for themselves on their own land. It was hard work all year long. Farmers cut and stored ice from the winter ponds to preserve milk and meat all summer; they chopped wood in January, tapped sugar maples in March, sheared sheep in April, fertilized garden and field corn in May, sowed in June, and cropped their hayfields all summer. Farm women canned or dried vegetables or stored them in cold cellars; they spun wool and wove cloth to make dresses, shirts, and trousers. Whole families pressed cider in autumn and all year long made their own soap and shoes, as well as ironwork in the home forge. Independence was everyone's vision, and each house a clapboard castle of liberty.

As the trains came, and the western plains provided farmland more suitable to newly invented machinery, small northern farms became difficult to sustain. From midcentury onward, young men and women drifted from the hills to work in factories. In the small town of Andover, New Hampshire, farm boys took jobs at a mill that used water power to manufacture hames (the wooden armature inside a horse collar) and enjoyed the short workweek (it seemed short to farmers) of twelve hours a day for six days. About 1900, when the mill cut down to half a day on Saturday, old-timers scoffed: "That's not a week's work."

By 1900 much of New Hampshire's population had gone south to textile mills along the Merrimack River, or west to Ohio or Minnesota or even Idaho and Oregon. New England's northern countryside emptied out, a landscape of collapsing barns and cellar holes in the woods where old roses and lilacs blossomed, memorials to generations of farm women. Their abandoned gardens still bloom as we approach the millennium.

As the twentieth century progressed, it was not only rural New England that depopulated itself. Even on the western plains, big farmers swallowed up small ones and agribusiness swallowed up big farmers. With the loss of the family farm came yearning for rural origins. In New Hampshire the children and grandchildren of farmers and gardeners returned to Old Home, and everywhere

in the United States city dwellers and suburbanites remembered what they missed or imagined they missed—land and landscape, independence and simplicity.

Some people moved back to the hills and plains. In New Hampshire people took summer vacations in places like Blackwater, and as they aged, some retired to their vacation houses. Others farmed in new ways, providing fresh vegetables to the summer people or concentrating on one crop, like apples or maple syrup. Others chose independence by opting for limited affluence, trading luxury for liberty. Ceramicists and woodworkers survive today in the hills where farm families once struggled and thrived.

In the future, maybe the computer, the fax, the modem—and goodness knows what else—will allow more people to return to the countryside, where they can conduct business from the wilderness as if they commuted regularly to a city office. Perhaps the shrunken cities will proclaim an Old Home Day so that nostalgic country dwellers may return to the places they started from.

—Donald Hall

The illustrations in this book were done in watercolor
on Arches paper with occasional pastel highlights.
The display and text type were set in Centaur.
Color separations by Bright Arts, Ltd., Singapore
Printed and bound by Tien Wah Press, Singapore
This book was printed with soya-based inks on Leykam recycled
paper, which contains more than 20 percent postconsumer
waste and has a total recycled content of at least 50 percent.
Production supervision by Warren Wallerstein and Ginger Boyer
Designed by Camilla Filancia